The Christmas Pony

Laura put her arms round Mr Crumbs's neck and hugged him. "I've decided what I'm going to do. I'm going to raise the money to keep him myself."

"How?" said Ben.

"There are loads of ways." She kissed Mr Crumbs on his soft nose. "I won't let you be sent away to strangers. They won't know where you like to be scratched or what your favourite treats are. I'm going to find a way to keep you – somehow."

Look out for more books by Sylvia Green!

Christmas Quackers
The Soft-Hearted Sheepdog
The Best Christmas Ever
A Parsnip Called Val

SYLVIA GREEN

The
Christmas Pony

Illustrated by Sharon Scotland

For Mr Crumbs – and Rosie
And for Laura and Emily

Scholastic Children's Books,
Commonwealth House, 1-19 New Oxford Street,
London WC1A 1NU, UK
a division of Scholastic Ltd
London ~ New York ~ Toronto ~ Sydney ~ Auckland
Mexico City ~ New Delhi ~ Hong Kong

Published in the UK by Scholastic Ltd, 2001

Text copyright © Sylvia Green, 2001
Illustrations copyright © Sharon Scotland, 2001
Cover illustration copyright © Mike Rowe, 2001

ISBN 0 439 99416 0

Printed by Cox & Wyman Ltd, Reading, Berks.

2 4 6 8 10 9 7 5 3 1

Chapter 1

Mr Crumbs

"Of course you can't have a pony for Christmas, Laura. We couldn't possibly afford one." Dad looked determined.

"But it's not just any pony – it's Mr Crumbs," said Laura. "And he's free to a good home."

"Ponies cost a fortune to keep," said Mum. "And apart from that we've got nowhere for him to live."

"We'd find somewhere—"

"No, Laura," said Dad. "You know how difficult things are at the moment."

"But if we can't give him a home he'll have to go and live at the horse and pony sanctuary," said Laura. "We'll never see him."

"I'm sorry, but the answer's still no," said Dad, in his don't-you-argue-with-me voice. "It's just not possible."

He went back out to the garage to finish the oil change on Mr Robert's Volvo and Mum went to answer the telephone.

"Told you they wouldn't agree," said Ben. "It's not practical."

Laura spun round to face her brother. "Oh, why do you always have to be so – so sensible."

"Probably 'cos I'm older than you."

"Only one year," said Laura.

"Dad's been really worried about money since he got made redundant," said Ben. "Especially as he had to take out that big bank loan to start the business."

"I know, I know – I had noticed," said Laura. Dad was always in his garage these days, repairing cars for people or out doing weddings in his vintage Daimler. And Mum spent most of her time in her workroom, making wedding dresses. "But there must be something we can do."

Laura marched out of the room feeling angry and frustrated. She couldn't just give up. She put on her coat and headed for the front door – a visit to Mr Crumbs always made her feel better.

She set off down the lane and soon

spotted Mr Crumbs. He was across the field socializing with the goats on the other side of the fence. He loved company. His sharp hearing immediately picked up Laura's footsteps and he raised his head and gave a loud whinny. With his ears pricked he trotted over to her.

The late November sun shone on his golden coat – it was the colour of toast crumbs, hence his name. Mr Crumbs was a Palomino pony – his pale mane and tail contrasted beautifully with his golden coat. He had a white blaze on his nose and a white stocking on one of his hind legs.

Laura closed the gate behind her and smiled up at the pony.

"Hello, Crumbs." She stroked his warm, broad forehead, but he immediately tried to push his large nose into her pocket, eager to find out if she had something for him.

Laura laughed as he nudged her. "Steady on. You'll knock me over." She took out the ready-sliced carrot and gave him a piece.

He watched her with his velvet-brown

eyes as he crunched on his favourite treat. Then he tilted his head and peered out of the corner of his eye to see if she had any more carrot in her other hand. Ben called that his "quizzical look".

Laura laughed and gave him the second piece. "There's no fooling you, is there!" She loved the feel of his silky-soft muzzle on her hand as he quickly searched out the carrot and gently took it. Mr Crumbs never failed to cheer her up, but this time she couldn't help feeling a little sad.

"I'm afraid Mum and Dad said no," Laura told him, as she patted his firm shoulder. "But don't you worry, I'll think of a way to keep you."

Mr Crumbs tossed his head, shaking his long mane, and blew gently down his nostrils. Laura couldn't imagine life without him. For as long as she could remember he'd been there, in his field. They passed him on their way into town, and on their way to school. At first they'd just stopped to talk to him every day, and sometimes have a chat with Mrs Cox, his owner.

Gradually they'd spent more and more time with him. Then a year ago Mrs Cox had been ill, and Laura and Ben had helped look after Mr Crumbs. When she was better they'd continued to help and in return she'd taught them both to ride him. But now Mrs Cox was moving to Australia to live near her daughter, and a leisure centre was going to be built on her house and land. She had to find a new home for Mr Crumbs before she left.

"Mrs Cox says no one will buy you because you're too old," said Laura.

"I don't think you're old – you're only eighteen. You could easily live till you're twenty-five."

She reached up to scratch him between his ears, under his forelock, and Mr Crumbs bent his head towards her. Next to carrots, his favourite thing in life was a good scratch under his forelock.

She heard the gate click and turned to see Ben.

"Hello, Crumbs," said Ben, reaching up to pat him on his glossy neck.

Mr Crumbs greeted him with a soft whinny.

"Mrs Cox says they're very kind at the horse and pony sanctuary," said Ben. "And he'll have lots of company."

"But it's miles and miles away. We'll never see him," said Laura. "I thought you wanted to keep him too."

"I do." Ben adjusted his glasses with his free hand. "You know I do – but I can understand the reasons why we can't."

Tiggy, Mrs Cox's cat, strolled over to them and Mr Crumbs put his head down to greet her.

"He's going to miss Tiggy – and the goats – as well as Mrs Cox," said Laura. "I can't bear the thought of him missing us too."

She put her arms round Mr Crumbs's neck and hugged him. "I've decided what I'm going to do. I'm going to raise the money to keep him myself."

"How?"

"There are loads of ways."

"Such as?"

"Oh, loads and loads of ways – I'll think of something."

She kissed Mr Crumbs on his soft nose. "I won't let you be sent away to strangers. They won't know where you like to be scratched or what your favourite treats are. I'm going to find a way to keep you – somehow."

Chapter 2

The Mr Crumbs Committee

"Emily says she'll help me raise the money," said Laura. "And she's offered to help look after Mr Crumbs."

"What does Emily know about looking after a pony?" said Mum. "I know she's your best friend, but this isn't a game. It's a big commitment."

"She knows that," said Laura. "She's been with me to visit Mr Crumbs lots of times and she loves him too. I'll teach her how to look after him."

"Emily's mum won't have any money to spare for a pony," said Dad.

"I told you. We're going to raise the money ourselves," said Laura. "Emily's coming round in a minute to discuss it."

"All right. You find out how much it costs to keep a pony," said Dad. "Then, if you can raise enough money in advance to keep Mr Crumbs for at least six months – and find somewhere to keep him – we'll think about it."

Laura was over the moon. Things were looking hopeful. But as her parents left the room she heard Dad whisper to Mum. "She's just a kid," he said. "She'll never do it – not six months' money in advance. We're quite safe."

"How dare he call me 'just a kid'," Laura complained to Ben. "And how dare he say I'll fail before I've even started."

"No, that was unfair," said Ben. "It even made me cross."

"Then why don't you help us?" said Laura. "Let's prove to Dad and Mum that we can do it. We can own Mr Crumbs between the three of us – you, me and Emily."

Ben took his glasses off, polished them on his jumper and put them back on again. "Well, I suppose we could just do a business plan and see if it might work."

"A what?"

"A business plan. Like Dad did when he was setting up the business. It's what all good businesspeople do to see if their ideas are practical."

"But we're not a bus –" Laura started,

but quickly stopped herself. Maybe it was a good idea – especially if it meant that Ben would help…

As soon as Emily arrived, they all sat down at the kitchen table.

"This is so exciting," said Emily, shaking back her long dark hair. "I can't believe that we might own Mr Crumbs by Christmas."

"Now hold on, don't get too excited," Ben warned her. "It might not be practical. It's a pretty big thing, owning a pony."

"We can do it," said Laura. "I know we can."

"Well, the first thing is to see if it's possible," said Ben. He had just put his calculator on the table and opened his notebook when there was a knock on the back door.

Ben's friend, Sanjay, popped his head round it. "Hiya! You ready to go, Ben?"

Ben jumped up. "Sorry, Laura, I'm off. We're going out on our bikes."

"You can't leave yet," said Laura. "We've only just started."

"Started what?" said Sanjay, shutting the door behind him.

Ben explained about Mr Crumbs.

"Don't you want to keep him then?" asked Sanjay. "I think it would be fantastic to own a pony."

"It's not that I don't want to keep him," said Ben. "I just don't think it will work."

"Well, I'd certainly want to give it a try if it were me," said Sanjay. "I've always fancied having my own pony."

Laura thought quickly. "Would you like to join us, Sanjay? It'd be better with four people – cheaper for all of us."

"Wow! That'd be amazing," said Sanjay, grabbing a seat and drawing it up to the table. "Imagine – owning Mr Crumbs."

"Brilliant!" said Laura. "Let's get started." Another advantage of Sanjay joining them was that there were now three different families involved. If any of them were on holiday – or ill – there would always be someone to look after Mr Crumbs.

"I thought we could call ourselves The Mr Crumbs Committee," said Laura.

"Great," said Emily.

Ben opened his notebook. He wrote THE MR CRUMBS COMMITTEE and listed their names. "We need to work out how much money we think we can raise, and how much it will cost to keep him. And don't forget we haven't got much time. Mrs Cox is moving just after Christmas."

"Christmas is only four-and-a-half weeks away," said Emily.

"Exactly," said Ben.

They started by discussing their pocket money. Laura and Ben got two pounds fifty a week each. Emily got two pounds and Sanjay got four pounds a week, as he helped with recycling all the packaging in his dad's chemist's shop.

After some discussion, they decided it would be fair to put one pound a week each into the fund. They would all need some money to themselves – for Christmas presents, sweets and CDs – and Ben was saving up for a computer.

"Right, fundraising," said Laura. "I thought car-cleaning – we might get some business from Dad's clients."

"Dog-walking," said Sanjay.

"Shopping," said Ben.

"Snow-clearing," said Emily.

They all looked at her. "But it's not snowing."

"It might. If it gets a bit colder," said Emily. "I love snow."

Ben wrote it all down. "We could charge two pounds for everything we do. Keep it simple."

He quickly worked out that if they each did one job a week – for two pounds – and added the one pound from their pocket money, the total between them would be twelve pounds a week.

"That should be plenty – surely," Laura said.

"Well, the next thing is to find out how much it will cost to keep Mr Crumbs," said Ben.

"There's his food," said Laura.

"Vet's bills," said Sanjay.

"Bedding?" said Emily.

"And rent – if we can find somewhere to keep him," said Ben.

"What about the field with Maggie's goats on?" suggested Sanjay.

"That's been bought up for the leisure centre too," said Ben. "Maggie's moving down to Sussex and taking the goats with her."

"We'll soon find somewhere else," said Laura.

Ben listed everything down. "When we've found out all the information we'll be able to see if it will be practical."

Laura smiled to herself. Of course it would be "practical". It was going to work out – she just knew it was.

Chapter 3

Making Plans

Later that afternoon, the four friends met up at Mrs Cox's and Laura gave Emily her first lesson on grooming.

Mr Crumbs loved being groomed. He closed his eyes and gave a low snicker as Laura worked over his neck with the dandy brush.

Laura smiled. "That's his favourite bit."

"He's gorgeous," said Emily, patting his glossy shoulder.

Laura showed her how to brush Mr Crumbs's beautiful mane and tail with the body brush. She brushed each of his legs and then gave him a drink of water.

The pony looked up expectantly as Ben arrived back with his food bucket. He pawed the ground impatiently until it was given to him. Sanjay carried the hay net and the two boys hung it up in the stable.

Mrs Cox arrived with mugs of hot chocolate for them all. "I'm thrilled to bits about your plans to keep Mr Crumbs," she told them. "I do hope it works out. I'll be much happier knowing that I'm leaving him with people he loves – and who love him."

She didn't think it was impossible at all. Laura and Ben had proved how well they could look after Mr Crumbs during the past year. The only thing she insisted on was that they all had their parents' permission and that they found secure premises to keep him in – with supervision from an experienced adult. "However capable I know you are," she said, "I'm afraid I can't just hand Mr Crumbs over to you."

As they sipped their drinks they watched Mr Crumbs munching intently in his large bucket, sorting out the carrots to eat first. Gradually an orange, slobbery mess formed round his mouth.

Laura chuckled. "That's why I leave washing his muzzle until last."

"Good thinking!" said Mrs Cox, laughing. "Now, you asked about the cost of keeping him. I've done a few quick calculations. There's his compound mix, vitamins, hay – oh, and his carrots."

She smiled at her pony's orange lips. "We mustn't forget his carrots. So, all his food, and straw for his bedding, adds up to about ten pounds a week."

Ben whipped out his notebook and wrote it down.

"Then there's his shoes."

Laura sighed. They'd forgotten about shoes. It was already going to cost more than she'd thought.

"Mr Norris comes every six to eight weeks and does them for me for forty-five pounds," said Mrs Cox.

"Forty-five pounds?" said Emily. "Every six to eight weeks? Why?"

"It's very important that Mr Crumbs has new shoes, and his feet trimmed regularly," Mrs Cox explained. "Otherwise he could get sore feet, or even damage them."

"Oh, I see," said Emily.

"Then there's vet's bills," Mrs Cox continued. "Including worming, vaccinations and having his teeth checked regularly. It's difficult to put a figure on that, it depends what needs treating at the time."

Ben tapped away on his calculator. "Food, bedding and shoes comes to approximately eight hundred and thirty-five pounds a year. That's about sixteen pounds a week. Plus we need to put something aside for vet's bills."

"We're only going to have twelve pounds," said Emily. "It's not enough."

Laura sighed but she wasn't going to be put off. "We can do two jobs a week each," she said quickly. "That'll bring in another eight pounds."

"Two jobs is the maximum," said

Sanjay. "We've got to leave time to see to Mr Crumbs and do our homework. And don't forget I have to help my dad, too."

"Two jobs each brings it up to twenty pounds a week," said Ben. "We'd be okay for his keep – and probably the vet's bills. But there's still his accommodation. We don't know how much that's going to cost."

"I'll make some enquiries for you," said Mrs Cox. "I'm sure we can find somewhere nearby to keep him."

"I do hope so," said Laura, gently washing Mr Crumbs's nose and muzzle with a sponge.

Then Ben untied him, led him into the stable and took his head collar off.

Tiggy immediately jumped up on to the stable door. Mr Crumbs came over to greet the tabby cat and she rubbed herself against his nose before jumping down and settling in the straw.

"Mrs Worth at the post office has offered to take Tiggy in," said Mrs Cox. "But Tiggy and Crumbs are really going to miss each other."

Laura wondered if they could find a way to keep them together, but she didn't say anything – not yet.

Mrs Cox picked up the empty mugs. "If there's anything I can do to help, let me know," she said, and headed indoors.

Laura and Ben picked up a shovel and a bucket.

"Right," said Ben. "Now for the fun job! We've got to pick up his droppings from the field. We have to keep it clean."

"Manure!" cried Emily.

"Er – yes, Emily," said Sanjay. "That *is* what it's called."

"No, silly. What I mean is – my Uncle Jack buys manure from the garden centre to put on his allotment," said Emily. "And so do lots of other people. We could sell the manure to raise money."

"Brilliant," said Laura, laughing. "What do you think you can manage, Mr Crumbs? A bucketful a day?"

Mr Crumbs tossed his head and walked over to his hay net.

"You've embarrassed him now," said Sanjay.

Ben was making notes. "We could probably get between twenty-five and fifty pence a bucket for it," he said. "I bet we could earn one or even two pounds a week. Well done, Emily, that's a great idea."

Emily beamed at him.

"We need to think up more ideas like that," said Sanjay, as they headed for the field. "Our biggest problem is going to be raising six months' money up front. We haven't got much time."

Laura thought about it as they went about their task. It would be difficult, as Mr Crumbs had to be re-homed shortly after Christmas. There were only four-and-a-half weeks to Christmas, and if they were lucky they might have one or two weeks afterwards.

"What we need is a big money-making idea," said Ben.

"How about putting on a Christmas show?" Emily suggested.

But the others weren't keen – they thought it would be too complicated.

Then Laura had a brainwave. "A

Christmas Bazaar!" she cried. "We can make things – and collect stuff from other people to sell."

"That's a great idea," said Emily, as they hurried back to the stable. "I bet we'd make lots of money."

Mr Crumbs heard them come back and put his head over the stable door to join in the conversation.

"We'll need somewhere to hold it," said Sanjay, patting the pony's neck. "A hall or something."

"Halls cost money to hire," said Ben.

"It needs to be somewhere cheap," said Laura. "Somewhere cheap – and different."

"Something like a big shed, or a barn?" said Emily.

"A barn would be great," said Laura. "We could decorate it and make it really Christmassy."

Mr Crumbs tossed his head and gave a little whinny. He obviously agreed.

"That old man next door to you's got a barn," said Sanjay. "D'you think he'd let us use it?"

"I dunno," said Laura. "But it's worth a try." Mr Jakes had lived next door to them for about six months, but they hardly ever saw him. His house was a converted farm cottage and in his back garden was a big, old barn that had been on the land when he bought it from the farmer. He sometimes said hello to Mum or Dad but he always seemed very unfriendly towards the children, and avoided them whenever possible.

"I can't imagine he uses the barn for anything," said Laura. "And surely for a good cause like this…"

"We'll go and ask him tomorrow morning," said Ben. "After we've seen to Mr Crumbs."

Chapter 4

Mr Jakes

"I'm not usually up this early on a Sunday morning," said Emily, yawning, as they put the stable-cleaning equipment away.

Laura smiled. "You'll get used to it."

They started down the drive and paused by the gate to the field. Mr Crumbs was concentrating hard in his efforts to pull the hay out of the hay net they'd hung up for him. He swung his head round to them, chewing thoughtfully.

Laura scratched him under his forelock. "Your stable's all done, so we're off now. See you this evening, Crumbs."

Sanjay stroked him. "Doesn't he get cold out here?"

"No, his coat is nice and thick, and it hasn't been clipped," said Ben. "But if it gets really cold we put a rug on him."

"Oh, right," said Sanjay, as they left. "Well, Emily, we've had our first lesson in mucking out."

"Yeah, we're learning fast," said Emily. "I'm so glad my mum okayed it for me to own him with you three. Even if she did agree with Ben and Laura's dad that we had to get at least six months' money up front."

"My mum and dad were actually quite keen," said Sanjay. "They said the responsibility would do me good."

"I'm really glad they agreed too," said Ben. "If this is going to be possible, it'll need the four of us."

"Of course it's going to be possible," said Laura. "Now come on, let's go and ask Mr Jakes about his barn."

There was no answer when they knocked on Mr Jakes' front door.

They tried round the back but there was no sign of him there either.

"He's probably gone out," said Sanjay.

"Let's have a quick peek inside the barn," suggested Emily. "We might be able to see what it looks like."

They had just reached the barn when the door opened and Mr Jakes came hurrying out. "What are you kids up to?" he shouted.

Ben, Emily and Sanjay all jumped back, but Laura stood her ground. "Good morning, Mr Jakes," she said. "We were – er – just wondering if we could use your barn for our Christmas Bazaar."

"I don't want kids round here, causing trouble," said Mr Jakes, hastily pulling the barn door closed behind him. "Clear off."

"But—"

"There's nothing here to interest you. Don't come near my barn again."

"What an unfriendly man," said Emily, as they hurried away.

"Why's he so touchy about an old barn?" asked Sanjay.

"Maybe he's a bank robber," said Emily. "And he's got all his loot stashed away in there. He looks like a crook – he's got shifty eyes."

"Well, we've got more important things to worry about than him," said Laura.

"Such as where else to hold our bazaar – and where we can keep Mr Crumbs," said Sanjay. "Obviously no point in asking Mr Jakes if he can live in his barn."

"Wouldn't be any good anyway," said Ben. "Mr Crumbs needs at least an acre of field to be turned out into during the day."

"There must be loads of other places," said Laura. "Like – like the farm next door. They must have got another barn if they sold this one to Mr Jakes."

"Okay, we'll go and ask," said Ben.

They trudged next door, trying to remain cheerful. But the farmer didn't have a barn they could use for the bazaar. And neither did he have any land he could rent out for Mr Crumbs to live on. Even Emily's offer of free manure towards the rent couldn't sway him.

They headed off home for lunch. It wasn't a very good start to the day, but they all had fundraising plans for the afternoon. Sanjay had arranged for him and Ben to wash his dad's car for two pounds. Emily was going to walk a neighbour's dog. And Laura had offered to do some housework for an elderly friend of her mum's.

They agreed to meet afterwards to get Mr Crumbs in for the night and to discuss how they'd got on.

Laura was the first to arrive. Mr Crumbs immediately left his pow-wow with the goats and trotted over to her. She slipped the lead-rope round his neck and gave him a piece of apple.

"Good boy," she said, as she slid the headcollar over his nose. She lifted the strap behind his ears and buckled it up. "You're such a good boy."

Laura walked alongside his head and led him over to the stable. "We haven't found anywhere to keep you yet – but we've got loads more ideas," she told him.

Tiggy greeted them outside the stable and Laura fetched the grooming kit. She took out the hoof pick and ran her hand down Mr Crumbs's front leg to his fetlock. He obediently lifted his foot so she could pick out his hoof. "I wonder where the others have got to?" she said. "I'm dreading telling them how much I earned this afternoon."

Laura had finished grooming Mr Crumbs and was giving him his drink of water by the time Ben and Sanjay arrived. They held out four pound coins. "We washed two cars," said Sanjay. "One of my neighbours saw us washing Dad's car and asked us to do hers as well."

"How much did you get, Laura?" Ben asked.

It was time to own up. "Ten pence."

"Ten pence?"

Laura explained how she'd cleaned the whole of the lady's kitchen, including the cooker. Then the old lady had thanked her and given her ten pence. "I don't know if she didn't hear me properly or if she hadn't got any money," said Laura. "But I didn't like to ask for more."

Ben laughed. "Let's hope Emily did better." He went off with Sanjay to get Mr Crumbs's food.

But Emily arrived with no money. The dog she was walking had run off and she'd had to get the owner to help find it. So of course, he hadn't paid her.

Ben did a quick calculation while Mr Crumbs noisily searched out the carrots in his bucket of food. With the one pound contribution each from their pocket money, they had raised eight pounds and ten pence. "We've got a long way to go," he said.

Laura sighed. "Let's go home and start working out what we can make for our bazaar."

"Okay," said Ben. "We'll have a meeting of the Mr Crumbs Committee on Wednesday evening and see what we've all come up with."

Mr Crumbs finished his food and Laura washed his nose and orange lips with the sponge. "Don't worry, this is only the first weekend," she whispered to him, as she led him into his stable. "There's still loads of time."

He gave a little whinny and she was sure he understood her.

Chapter 5

We Can't Give up

They had a half-day off school on Wednesday so Laura took the opportunity of an extra ride on Mr Crumbs. During the winter she usually only got to ride him at weekends, because it got dark so early.

Emily was doing some shopping for an elderly neighbour and Ben and Sanjay had gone to have a chat with Mrs Cox.

Laura liked her time alone with Mr Crumbs. She gave him a gentle squeeze with her legs. "Walk on, Mr Crumbs."

He obediently set off round the field. Somehow the field, and the surrounding area, looked different from between Mr Crumbs's ears. It was as though she was seeing it from his view.

She gave him another squeeze. "Trot on, Mr Crumbs."

They trotted round for a while and then slowed to a walk. Mrs Cox was happy for Laura to exercise Mr Crumbs on her own. She knew she could trust her just to stay in the field. Laura's riding hat had been a birthday present, and Mrs Cox had given her and Ben riding boots that had belonged to her children.

Laura brought Mr Crumbs to a halt. She leaned forward to pat his neck.

"That was great. Good boy." She slipped her feet out of the stirrups and dismounted.

"We're having a meeting of the Mr Crumbs Committee tonight," she told him, as she ran the stirrups up the stirrup leathers. Then she slackened the girth. "Ben wants to talk about his business plan and we're going to discuss our ideas for the bazaar."

She led him off towards the stable. "But we haven't found anywhere to hold the bazaar yet. The village hall is much too expensive – and in any case it's booked. And so are both the church halls."

Laura tied Mr Crumbs up and took his saddle off. "But the rest of the fundraising's going quite well. Ben washed one of Dad's client's cars yesterday and I cleaned the inside. We got two pounds each. Sanjay earned two pounds for cleaning his dad's shop window and Emily should get two pounds today."

Mr Crumbs tilted his head, peering out of the corner of his eye to see if any food was coming yet.

Laura loved it when he did that. She laughed and gave him a carrot. "We've already found a customer for your manure," she said, as his soft lips searched her hand to make sure he didn't miss any bits. "Emily's uncle. And he knows lots of other people with allotments."

Sanjay arrived and said that Ben had gone straight home to work on his business plan. He helped Laura groom and feed Mr Crumbs and clean the riding tack. Then they headed home, both looking forward to the meeting that evening.

Ben spread his papers in front of him on the table. He took his glasses off and polished them on his jumper. "I don't think we can do it."

"What?" Laura looked at him in horror.

"It's just not practical," said Ben, replacing his glasses. "Mrs Cox has been asking around and she says the very cheapest accommodation we're likely to find – just a field and basic shelter – is ten pounds a week."

"Not that she's found any that's available," said Sanjay. "And neither have we."

"Therefore, with ten pounds a week for food and bedding, six pounds towards shoeing, two pounds – at least – towards vet's bills and ten pounds for accommodation, if we can find any, that makes twenty-eight pounds a week," said Ben. "We can't earn twenty-eight pounds a week."

"But that's twenty-eight pounds between four of us," said Laura. "Seven pounds each."

"I can give an extra one pound a week," said Emily. "Mum got a pay rise and she said if I keep my bedroom clean and tidy she'll give me another one pound a week pocket money."

"And I don't mind making my contribution three pounds," said Sanjay. "As I get more than the rest of you."

"Well, I'm perfectly happy to give two pounds a week from my pocket money," said Laura. "There's nothing I want to spend my money on more than Mr Crumbs."

Ben wrote it all down and reluctantly agreed to raise his to one pound fifty. "That makes eight pounds fifty a week," he said.

"And the manure," said Emily.

"Okay, let's say an average of one pound fifty a week for the manure," said

Ben. "So that's ten pounds a week plus what we earn."

"And at two jobs a week each that's another sixteen pounds," said Laura. "So that's twenty-six pounds a week – we're almost there. We could make the bazaar an annual event to raise the rest of the money."

Ben did some more calculations. "We'll need to make at least a hundred and four pounds profit from the bazaar every year. But don't forget we've got to raise the first six months' money in just a few weeks. That's around seven hundred pounds. I just don't see how we can do that."

"Oh, for goodness' sake, let's at least try!" said Laura. She ran up to her room and came back with her piggy bank. "I was saving for a new bike but I want Mr

Crumbs more." The coins clattered all over the table as she shook it.

Ben counted it out. "Twenty-seven pounds and sixteen pence."

"I'll ask for money for Christmas instead of a present," said Laura. "And for my next birthday. And I don't care how hard I have to work. I don't want anything except Mr Crumbs. We can't give up."

"I don't want to give up," said Emily.

"No, let's give it a bit longer," said Sanjay.

"All right," said Ben. "We'll keep trying for a while. I suggest we open a savings account at the bank to keep the money in. At least it will be earning some interest."

"Good idea," said Laura. "Now what about the bazaar? I've got my list of ideas here." She took out a piece of paper.

"I thought we could cut out gift tags from old Christmas cards, and make tree decorations – I've seen some ideas in a magazine. Make fluffy spiders and chicks out of old wool, and have a Guess the Number of Sweets in the Jar competition."

"Great," said Emily. "Me next. I thought of making fudge and coconut ice – Mum's got some really easy recipes. Making peg bags, and having a lucky dip – we can buy some little gifts cheap from the market and wrap them up. And we could sell refreshments."

"I thought of painting some ordinary cheap pots to plant bulbs in," said Sanjay. "And I could make paperweights, plaster models and table decorations."

"And perhaps you could design some posters to advertise the bazaar, Sanjay," said Ben. "As you're the one that's best at artistic-type things." Then he got out his own list. "Christmas cards," he read. "Buying up large boxes from the market and putting them into nice smaller packages. And doing the same with wrapping paper. And we could sell second-hand books, videos and CDs that we can collect from friends and neighbours."

"Brilliant," said Laura. "And perhaps Mr Crumbs could give pony rides."

"Good idea. We could charge fifty pence a ride," said Ben. "I'll make a note of all the ideas and how much we could charge."

"There's only four weeks to Christmas," said Sanjay. "So we'd better get a move on."

"Yes. This has got to be the biggest and best bazaar ever," said Laura. "It's got to make loads and loads of money."

Chapter 6

More Ideas

On Saturday morning Laura and Emily met up to see to Mr Crumbs while Ben and Sanjay delivered manure to the allotments. Mrs Cox usually saw to her pony on weekday mornings and the children came every evening after school and twice at weekends. Soon – when Mr Crumbs belonged to them – they would have to get up early to see to him before school as well. Laura couldn't wait.

Mr Crumbs pawed the ground, impatient for his feed. His warm breath rose like steam in the morning air.

Emily finished brushing his tail and wiped under his dock with a sponge. "It was a shame about Marsham Hall, wasn't it?" she said.

"Yes, I'd really got my hopes up about that," said Laura, as she gave Mr Crumbs his food bucket. Marsham Hall was a big house just outside town and the owner kept three horses of her own. "Such a pity she didn't have room for Mr Crumbs as well."

They'd also tried Church Farm, Westdene Farm and Mr Brown who ran a market garden – but they hadn't had any luck there either.

Emily giggled as she watched Mr Crumbs searching out the carrots in his bucket. "I love the way he does that," she said. "He's a real carrot-oholic."

Laura smiled and patted the pony's warm neck. "I hope Ben and Sanjay have some luck at the vet's when they've finished delivering the manure. A vet must have somewhere to keep large animals that have to stay in."

"Yes, and if not, they're bound to know of somewhere else we can keep him," said Emily. "They must know all the farmers round here."

Laura led Mr Crumbs out to his field and saw to his hay net and water while Emily made a start on mucking out the stable. On Saturday mornings they removed all the straw and disinfected the floor.

As soon as they'd finished, the two girls made their way to *Fowler's Family*

Restaurant. Sanjay's mum had suggested they might have a room they could use for their bazaar.

"I'm really sorry but I'm using the room for extra seating now," said Mr Fowler. "But I think it's great what you kids are trying to do. When you do find somewhere, I'll give you a voucher for a meal for two as a raffle prize."

"Wow, thanks," said Emily.

"Why don't you try the *Rose and Crown Inn?*" he suggested. "They've definitely got a functions room they let out."

But the landlord of the *Rose and Crown Inn* couldn't help them either. "We have got a room," he said. "But I'm afraid it's fully booked for Christmas parties until the end of January."

It was disappointing, but encouraged by the offer from the restaurant, Laura plucked up the courage to ask if he would consider donating a raffle prize.

"I'll give you two bottles of wine," said the landlord. "You'll have to get your parents to collect them though."

"A raffle's a great idea," said Laura, as they left. "You make lots of money with a raffle."

On the way home they called in at the hardware store (who said they couldn't give them anything) and then the greengrocer's, who promised them a basket of fruit.

As they arrived at Laura's house, Emily spotted Mr Jakes carrying two large boxes of "loot" into his barn. "Did you see the shifty way he looked around him? I bet he is a bank robber. Hey!" Emily grabbed Laura's arm. "D'you think there might be a reward for his capture?"

"A what?"

"A reward." Emily's eyes were shining. "Just think, it would solve all our money worries for Mr Crumbs."

"Oh, Emily, Mr Jakes couldn't possibly be a—" Laura started, but Emily wasn't listening.

"We ought to spy on him – see if we can get any evidence." Emily crept over to the hedge to peer through. She turned back suddenly, her eyes wide. "Hey! I just heard someone crying out. It came from the barn."

"Honestly, Emily, your imagination gets worse all the time," Laura giggled. "It was just a chicken. There are loads on the farm. Now come on."

She ushered her indoors and they found Ben and Sanjay in the kitchen looking through the adverts in the local paper. They hadn't had any luck at the vet's but the vet said they could advertise for somewhere to keep Mr Crumbs on his notice board.

"We thought about putting an advert in the paper as well," said Ben.

"And in my dad's chemist's shop window," said Sanjay. "And the post office."

"Great," said Laura. "Let's write some out after lunch."

"We've got to make ourselves a sandwich," said Ben. "Mum's doing a fitting for two bridesmaids in the living room."

"They must be the ones in red velvet," said Laura. "Mum was working on their dresses yesterday."

They heard the steady chug of Dad's vintage Daimler as it pulled up in the drive. He'd been to do a wedding over in Stanton, about twenty miles away.

Dad opened the kitchen door. "You kids couldn't do me a favour, could you? Wash and polish the Daimler? I've just driven down a really muddy lane and the car's got filthy."

"How much?" asked Laura. This was business, after all.

"A fiver, if you can do it right away," said Dad. "I need the car for another wedding at three o'clock, and I've got to fix Dr Johnson's BMW."

"Oh well, lunch will have to wait," said Ben, as they filled buckets with hot water and fetched old cloths. They started work on the muddy paintwork and Laura and Emily told the two boys about the raffle prizes.

"That's great," said Ben. "I've been doing some figures on the bazaar. The packets of gift tags we've made should sell for fifty pence each." He wiped the water splashes off his glasses with his sleeve. "So that's eighteen pounds if we sell all thirty-six packets. And the fluffy spiders and chicks could bring in twenty-five pounds – if we can make fifty."

Emily giggled. "Only if we can make the chicks look less like vultures."

"Tonight we ought to wrap up all those notebooks, pencils and plastic toys we got from the market for the lucky dip," said Sanjay.

"And we should make a start on the big boxes of Christmas cards," said Laura. "I thought we could put twelve in a packet and maybe stick tiny crêpe-paper bows on the front to make them look nice."

The car was soon washed and dried. The boys polished the paintwork while Laura and Emily started on the big chrome headlights.

Then they swept the confetti out of the interior and put fresh white ribbons on the front. It looked good when they'd finished. Even Dad was pleased – and he was very fussy.

"You've done a really good job," he said, handing a five-pound note to Ben.

Laura watched him reverse the car into the garage and had an idea. Dad's garage was big – not really as big as they wanted, but they could make do. "Dad, as you're out most Saturdays at weddings, could we use the garage for our bazaar?"

"No, Laura. Even if I have two weddings, like today, the car is back here at some point, and I need to keep it under cover," said Dad. "And there's usually a customer's car in the garage too."

"Shame, the garage would have been good," said Sanjay, as they went indoors. "But at least it's lunch time now – at last."

As they ate, they wrote out the advertisements for the vet's, the local newspaper, Sanjay's shop and the post office.

"What about the library?" said Sanjay. "They've got a noticeboard."

"Yes. And they might have a room for the bazaar," said Laura.

"Let's go there first then," said Ben. "There's only three-and-a-half weeks to Christmas now."

Chapter 7

A Breakthrough

Laura paused from sifting out the soiled straw with the fork to watch Mr Crumbs. Emily was sitting on him and Ben was leading her round the field.

He's so beautiful, she thought. *We've got to raise the money to keep him.*

They hadn't had any luck with a room for the bazaar at the library yesterday. But they had put up one of their notices asking for a field and stable.

Mrs Cox had got a date for moving out now – the eighth of January. So they had to find somewhere for Mr Crumbs to live before then.

Laura sighed and went back to forking up the straw. "Hey, mind out, Tiggy," she said, as she spotted the tabby cat curled up in the corner. "You don't want to be put on the muck heap, do you?"

Tiggy reluctantly got up, stretched herself and strolled outside.

Laura wheeled the full wheelbarrow round the back and had just put the fresh straw in the stable when Ben brought Emily back on Mr Crumbs. Laura held the pony's reins and stroked his nose while Ben helped Emily to dismount.

There was such trust in his velvet-brown eyes as he looked at her. "I won't let you down," she told him.

Laura took her hard hat from Emily and swung herself into the saddle.

She walked Mr Crumbs back to the field and leaned over and patted his strong neck. "There's still time to raise the money," she whispered to him. "And to find somewhere to keep you."

She gave him a gentle squeeze with her legs. "Trot on, Mr Crumbs."

They had a busy week. Every evening, after they'd seen to Mr Crumbs and had dinner, the four friends met up to work on things for their bazaar. But they still couldn't find anywhere to hold it.

Laura was glad when it was Friday – she was looking forward to spending time over the weekend with Mr Crumbs. She and Emily waited for Ben and Sanjay after school as they usually did, so they could all go together to see to Mr Crumbs.

But the boys were late coming out and Laura was getting impatient. "Where have they got to?" she asked Emily. "We've got to see to Mr Crumbs, and sew the legs on all those fluffy spiders for the bazaar later."

"They didn't say they weren't coming with us," said Emily.

Laura sighed and went back into school to look for them. She was tired – they were all tired.

She spotted Ben in the hall. His class was performing a nativity play for the rest of the school and they were obviously rehearsing.

Ben saw her and came to the door. "We'll be about another half an hour," he said. "You'd better go on without us."

"Why didn't you tell me you had a rehearsal?" Laura demanded. "Emily and I could almost have finished Mr Crumbs by now. And we've got loads more work to do this evening. There's only two-and-a-half weeks to Christmas now." She felt so tired and her head was beginning to ache.

"Sorry," said Ben. "I forgot."

"You forgot?" Laura snapped. "The trouble with you is that you don't really care, do you? Oh, you come along and do a few bits and pieces. And you write figures in your notebook. But you're not committed, are you?"

Laura didn't wait for an answer – she stormed out of the school to where Emily was waiting for her.

Emily did her best to cheer her friend up as they walked along to Mrs Cox's and

Laura had calmed down a bit by the time they got there. But Mr Crumbs always sensed when Laura wasn't happy. Emily was fixing the hay net in the stable and Laura went to untie the lead rope to take him inside.

Suddenly Mr Crumbs brought his head down and rested it on her shoulder. She reached up and stroked the side of his face. His warmth and familiar smell were comforting.

The two girls paused outside Laura's house and Laura even managed a smile when Emily spotted a ginger cat going into Mr Jakes's garden.

"I wouldn't go in there if I were you," Emily told it. "He'll probably eat you – or make you into fur gloves."

"Emily, that's awful," she giggled.

Emily left to go home for dinner and Laura went indoors and straight up to her room. It was full of things they'd made for the bazaar, as well as second-hand books and CDs they'd collected from friends and neighbours, and a Christmas cake Emily's mum had made them. Ben had decided they'd make more money from the cake if they asked people to guess the weight rather than just sell it.

They'd got a jar of sweets from the newsagents for people to guess how many there were. And *The Bookstore* had given them a book token for the raffle.

Laura slumped down on the bed and looked at the stacks of boxes. What was the use of it all if they hadn't got anywhere to hold the bazaar? For the first time, she felt really discouraged.

The door opened and Ben came

in. Laura ignored him – she was still feeling cross.

"How about the school hall to hold the bazaar in?" he said. "And for free?"

"What? I mean – how?" Laura wasn't sure she'd heard right. "You're not joking, are you?"

"No." Ben adjusted his glasses. "I thought about things after you'd gone. And how hard you'd worked – it's all down to you, really."

"Look, I'm sorry – about what I said," said Laura. "We've all worked really hard. I was tired and – oh, just tell me what happened."

"Well, I knew the school hall is only usually used for school events," said Ben. "But I thought it was worth a try, and I told Miss Featherstone all about Mr Crumbs."

"And she said we could use the hall? Just like that?" said Laura.

"Not quite 'just like that'," said Ben. "She was impressed with what we've been doing – and she just happens to love horses. So she went off and made a couple of phone calls and then came back to say it was all okay – for Saturday week. The fifteenth of December."

Chapter 8

Busy Days

The next day, Saturday, was really busy. All four of them spent the whole day working on things for the bazaar. But none of them felt tired any more.

When they went to bring Mr Crumbs in for the night, Laura and Ben left Emily and Sanjay to groom and feed him on their own while they cleaned up his field.

Both Emily and Sanjay were quite

competent now and the pony was happily sorting out the carrots in his food bucket when Laura and Ben returned.

"We've definitely reached a turning point now," said Sanjay.

Laura nodded and patted Mr Crumbs. "Bet you anything someone will ring this weekend and offer us a field and a stable."

"Yeah – for practically nothing as well," Emily chuckled.

Mr Crumbs finally lifted his nose out of the bucket and Sanjay gently washed it with the sponge.

The pony had picked up on their excitement and looked from one to the other. Then he tossed his head and whinnied.

Ben laughed and patted him. "It's great, your mums offering to do the refreshments at the bazaar," he said to Emily and Sanjay.

"Yeah, they got together this morning about it," said Sanjay. "My mum's making lots of different savouries and Emily's mum is making cakes."

"And they're going to serve tea and coffee, and orange juice," said Emily.

"That's great," said Laura, but she felt a bit awkward. Emily's and Sanjay's mums were helping and Sanjay's dad was donating a box of bath toiletries for the raffle. But her mum and dad hadn't offered anything.

Dad had been out doing a wedding today and she'd hardly seen Mum. The two bridesmaids with the red velvet dresses – and the bride – had been round in the morning for a final fitting and since then Mum had been shut away in her workroom. They were both obviously too busy to help.

Emily started to lead Mr Crumbs into the stable, but halfway there he resisted and turned to look at Laura.

Laura patted him. "Go on, Crumbs. Emily knows what she's doing."

Mr Crumbs obediently went inside and Emily took off his headcollar. She closed the half-door on the stable behind her and he hung his head over it so that he could be included. He hated to miss anything.

Mrs Cox arrived with their hot chocolate. "I'm so excited about your bazaar. It's really looking hopeful that you might be able to keep Mr Crumbs now," she told them. "Oh, I know the sanctuary would take good care of him but I'd much rather he stayed with you."

Laura smiled at her. "Thanks."

"I only wish I could help you out financially, but all my money's tied up in the move to Australia," said Mrs Cox. "But if you'd like any of the tack – saddles, bridles, that sort of thing – you're welcome to it. And all the stable-cleaning equipment."

"Wow, thanks," said Laura. "That'll be a terrific help."

The next week was spent in a frenzy of activity. They worked like crazy to finish off the things they were making. Mrs Cox was clearing out her house ready to move and she gave them more books and lots of bric-a-brac to sell. Emily's uncle promised them produce from his allotment and some plants from his greenhouse.

There was no doubt about Ben's commitment now. He spent hours making Christmas decorations to sell. He made bells, angels, Christmas trees and robins, which he cut out of card. Then he painted them, covered them in glitter and added thread to hang them up.

Laura and Emily bought dozens of hyacinth, crocus and daffodil bulbs from the market and planted them in Sanjay's brightly painted pots.

Sanjay painted banners and posters to advertise the bazaar. They put them up everywhere anyone would allow them to, including three in the school. He also painted some large stones with brightly-coloured patterns, to be used as paperweights.

They all made table decorations out

of logs and holly and Emily made fudge and coconut ice. Laura and Ben wrapped up another fifty lucky dips. They decorated a large box with crêpe paper, and filled it with shredded newspaper to hide the gifts.

On Friday evening everything was packed up and Sanjay's dad brought his car round to take it all to the hall. "Looks like this lot will take two trips," he said.

Then Emily's mum arrived to take Emily to pick up the raffle prizes they'd been promised.

Laura and Ben's dad was still in the garage and their mum was in her workroom – she'd hardly come out all week.

Laura and Ben called out to them as they left. "We're off to the school now." But they didn't come out to say goodbye.

Miss Featherstone was waiting for them at the hall. She seemed quite excited as she helped them carry in the boxes. "I can't believe how much stuff you've got," she said.

The caretaker had already put out tables for them, and Laura immediately started arranging the Christmas cards and gift tags on one of them.

They'd just finished unloading Sanjay's dad's car when, to everyone's surprise, Laura and Ben's mum and dad turned up too. Dad's car was piled up with the rest of their goods.

Mum and Dad unloaded everything from the car and helped arrange it on the tables. Just as they finished unpacking the last of the goods, Mum handed Laura a large box.

Laura opened it to see six dolls all

dressed as brides. Mum had used the leftover material from all the wedding dresses she'd made. Under a layer of tissue were eight soft Father Christmases, made from the leftover red velvet from the bridesmaids' dresses. So that's what she'd been doing all week.

"Oh, Mum." Laura flung her arms round her mother. "Thanks."

"And this," said Mum, handing her an envelope. "It's a voucher for your raffle. I talked Dad into giving a free ride in his Daimler."

Laura was overjoyed. Everything was going so well. Then an awful thought struck her. "S'posing," she said, "just supposing – no one comes."

Chapter 9

The Mr Crumbs Christmas Bazaar

They were up extra early on Saturday morning. Ben, Emily and Sanjay went straight to the school hall to put the finishing touches to the stalls and help set out the refreshments.

Laura went to see to Mr Crumbs and help Mrs Cox get him ready for the pony rides he was going to give at the bazaar.

He immediately sensed the excitement and they had trouble getting him to stand still while Laura painted hoof oil on his hooves to make them shiny.

Then he tried to eat the tinsel they were attaching to the browband at the top of his bridle.

"He probably thinks he's going to a gymkhana," Mrs Cox chuckled, as they entwined red and green ribbons into his mane and tail. "We used to enter him with the children when they were young."

Laura changed her clothes and packed some hay and his water bucket in a bag, along with plenty of carrots for treats during the day.

Then she mounted up and leaned forward to give Mr Crumbs a hug. "You're so smart. You're a real Christmas pony today."

Mrs Cox led him along the road as Laura had only ever ridden him in the field. Laura looked around her and, once again, was amazed at how different – how beautiful – the world looked from up on his back.

When they reached the school she was relieved to see lots of people waiting to go in. And a queue had already formed at the notice they'd put up for the pony rides.

"Isn't he beautiful," said one little girl, as they approached.

"I've got one pound," said a boy. "So I can have two rides."

Mrs Cox smiled. "I can see I'm going to be very busy today."

Laura dismounted and fetched Mr Crumbs some water. Then she gave him a special hug. "I love you, Mr Crumbs. Be a good boy today."

Hanging over the entrance to the hall was Sanjay's masterpiece. A huge banner which read:

THE MR CRUMBS CHRISTMAS BAZAAR
10'o clock today

Inside, the hall looked incredible with all the decorations up and the tables piled high with goods. Even though she'd seen it almost finished the night before it still took Laura's breath away.

"Is everyone ready?" she asked.

Everyone nodded or called out "yes" from behind their tables.

"Right, I'll open the doors." She took a deep breath. "This bazaar is now open," she declared.

The day passed in a haze of activity. All the children in the school must have come – and brought their parents.

All the bride dolls and the Father Christmases were sold very quickly. Laura noticed that several adults who bought them quickly hid them under their coats or in their bags – they were obviously Christmas presents.

Every time she looked up she could see Mr Crumbs going past the window with yet another child on his back. He really looked as though he was enjoying the company and all the attention.

Rebecca, who was in Laura's class, won the sweets by guessing how many were in the jar. And the butcher's wife guessed the correct weight of the Christmas cake.

The raffle was an incredible success

and made a hundred and two pounds. Mr Crumbs himself made twenty-five pounds. He could have made much more but Mrs Cox kept the number of rides down to fifty and made sure he had regular breaks.

There wasn't much left by the time they finally closed the doors. And all that remained on the refreshment table were empty plates and a couple of tea bags.

Ben went to help Mrs Cox take Mr Crumbs home and settle him for the night while the rest of them cleared up.

"Well done," said Miss Featherstone. "That was a big success. Do you think you've raised enough money?"

"We haven't counted it all yet," said Laura. "But thank you so much for helping and for arranging for us to use the hall."

"That's all right – I admire you for what

you're doing," said Miss Featherstone. "As I love horses myself, I can understand why you want to keep Mr Crumbs – he's a beautiful pony."

"I don't suppose there's anywhere to keep him here?" said Laura. "A field at the back of the school maybe? Everyone at school loved him today."

"I'd love to help but I'm afraid it's impossible. We can't keep Mr Crumbs on school property," said the teacher. "But I've been around horses for most of my life, so when you do find somewhere, if you need a hand with anything, I'd be pleased to help."

"Thanks," said Laura. "That's great." Now they had someone to go to for advice. And maybe Miss Featherstone could teach Emily and Sanjay to ride, and even help Laura and Ben improve their skills.

It was quite late by the time they got home but Ben wouldn't go to bed until they had counted all the money. They'd made an incredible five hundred and seventy-eight pounds and fifty pence profit. Added to what they'd already saved they now had six hundred and eighty-three pounds and seventy-six pence. Almost enough for six months' keep.

Laura tumbled into bed, exhausted. But she knew she wouldn't sleep, her mind was too active. They were almost there – if only they could find somewhere to keep Mr Crumbs. If only someone would read one of their adverts and ring about a field and shelter for him.

They were bound to ... it would happen next week ... their luck was turning after all.

Chapter 10

Christmas Eve

School broke up for Christmas on Wednesday and the four friends concentrated their efforts on finding somewhere to keep Mr Crumbs. The success of the bazaar had renewed their enthusiasm. They looked everywhere – asked everyone they could think of. They inquired at the council offices, the railway station, the water board – any place they thought could possibly have any land.

But there was nothing. And nobody phoned about their adverts.

"We're surrounded by fields," said Laura. "I can't believe there's not one we can use for Mr Crumbs. Not even one he can share."

So they started looking further away. The one place they found was the riding stables over at Westhorpe. But they only did full board at a hundred pounds a week. Even Laura agreed that was impossible.

By Christmas Eve they were feeling very low. They'd never dreamed it would be so hard to find Mr Crumbs a new home. And Mrs Cox was leaving for Australia in two weeks. Time was running out.

At lunchtime it started snowing and everyone felt even more depressed – except for Emily. "We'll be able to earn more money now, snow-clearing," she explained.

The snow shower didn't last long but it was heavy and covered everything in a soft white blanket.

They decided to go and see to Mr Crumbs a bit earlier that afternoon, to groom him and put his blanket on before it snowed again.

They trudged wearily up to his field. Mr Crumbs didn't hear them approach as he usually did because their footsteps were muffled by the snow. He was standing there looking really dejected.

"He's probably missing the goats," said Ben. "Maggie took them down to Sussex with her two days ago."

"Plus he senses that something's wrong," said Laura. It broke her heart to see him like this.

At the sound of their voices Mr Crumbs pricked up his ears. He tossed his head, whinnied loudly, and trotted over.

Sanjay put on his headcollar and gave him some cut-up apple. Then he led him over to the stable.

Laura started to pick out his hooves with the hoof pick while Sanjay went to see to his feed. Ben took Emily to fetch his stable rug as it had turned so cold.

"We've made our seven hundred pounds," Laura told Mr Crumbs. "Seven hundred and two pounds and thirty-four pence to be exact. Ben put Saturday's pocket money straight into the bank today."

She fetched the grooming brushes and started brushing the pony's golden coat with the dandy brush. He turned to look at her and she felt his warm, sweet breath on her face.

"All we need now is somewhere to keep you," said Laura, trying to sound cheerful. "There's probably somewhere really obvious that we just haven't thought of yet."

She moved round in front of him. Mr Crumbs's dark velvet eyes were sad. "I can't fool you, can I?" she said. "You're too intelligent. You know things aren't looking too hopeful right now."

Mr Crumbs rested his head on Laura's shoulder.

Laura put her arms round his neck and they stood there for a while, enjoying each other's warmth and comfort.

"Don't worry, I won't let you go," said Laura.

"You might have to," Ben warned her, as he and Emily came back with the stable rug. "There just isn't anywhere to keep him."

Laura didn't answer. She knew she'd burst into tears if she did.

It was snowing quite heavily again by the time they left Mr Crumbs. They trudged homewards and paused outside Ben and Laura's house to say goodbye. "Looks like Mum and Dad are still out Christmas shopping," said Ben. "The car's not here—" He stopped as they heard a shout.

"It came from Mr Jakes's house," said Emily. "What's he up to?"

"Oh, I can't be bothered with him right now," said Ben.

"Just ignore him, Emily," said Laura wearily.

The shout came again.

"He's calling for help," said Sanjay.

They immediately ran round to see Mr Jakes lying in his drive.

"I slipped on the snow," he cried. "I think I've broken my leg."

They rushed to help him. His head was bleeding and his leg was twisted in a most peculiar position. "Can you sit up?" asked Emily, bending down to him.

He waved her away. "Don't bother with me. Get help for the dog."

They all looked at each other in surprise. They didn't know he had a dog.

"What dog?" Laura asked.

"In the barn," he said. "She's giving birth – but she's in difficulties. Get some help."

The four children raced round to the barn. The door was open and they cautiously peered inside.

As their eyes became accustomed to the darkness they could see a black dog lying on a bed of straw. And there was more...

"Look, in that cage over there," said Laura, as they ventured in. "It's an owl."

"With one eye," said Sanjay. "And look, over there. A rabbit – and a pigeon."

Something scurried to the side of a run in the corner. "A fox," breathed Ben. "And his leg is bandaged."

An elderly-looking ginger cat came to greet them and rubbed round their legs.

"It's the one you saw coming in here, Emily," said Laura.

Something was snoring in a box under a table and a chicken squawked from the other side of the barn. "And that's the chicken I heard," said Emily.

"What are they all doing here?" said Sanjay, as the owl winked at him with its one eye.

"I don't know." Laura kneeled down beside the trembling dog. "But look at this poor dog. She really needs help."

Ben looked outside. "The back door of the house is open. I'll go and phone for some help."

Laura went back to see Mr Jakes. He was trying to drag himself up the drive on his bottom.

"You shouldn't move that leg," said Laura.

"Don't fuss about me," snapped the old man. "I told you to get help for the dog."

Ben appeared. "It's all under control. I've phoned for an ambulance for you," he told the old man. "And I've called a vet for the dog."

"What?" said Mr Jakes. "I'm not going to hospital. My animals need me – I can't just leave them. And I can't afford to have a vet come out. They charge a fortune for a call-out – and for an emergency. And this is both. Can't you get your parents to help or something?"

"Our parents are out," said Ben. "And we can't waste time trying to find someone who just might be able to help.

That dog needs a vet," he added firmly. "And she needs one now."

"And we'll look after the animals if you have to stay in hospital," said Laura.

"You? You're just kids," said Mr Jakes. "I'm not letting you anywhere near my animals."

Sanjay put his hands on his hips indignantly. "We're not 'just kids'. And we know all about looking after ponies – so your smaller animals and a couple of birds shouldn't be a problem."

Ben took out his notebook and pencil. "We know about cats, dogs and chickens. Just tell us what to do with the others."

Mr Jakes winced in pain. "I suppose I haven't really got a choice – like this. I'll have to trust you." He quickly told them how to care for the owl, rabbit, fox and pigeon. The hedgehog – which was what the snoring from the box under the table was – was hibernating and wouldn't need any attention. "You will treat them kindly, won't you?" he added.

"Of course we will," said Emily.

"But I've got no money at all to pay the vet," said Mr Jakes. "I bet it will cost at least a hundred pounds – maybe more."

Laura looked down at him. His eyes were moist. And it wasn't from the pain – he really cared about his animals. He wasn't a horrible man like they'd thought at all. She shifted her feet. "We've got some money," she said quietly.

"But that's for Mr Crumbs," said Ben.

Chapter 11

Give the Kids a Chance

Mr Jakes was just being carried into the ambulance when the vet arrived. The decision to pay for him with some of their money hadn't taken long to make. They couldn't let the poor dog suffer and they knew it was important to move fast.

And as Emily said, they'd have a week and a half after Christmas to earn some more money. "We'll just have to work extra hard. "At least we can do some snow-clearing."

"It'll mean less time to look for somewhere for Mr Crumbs to live," said Ben. "Especially now we've got to look after Mr Jakes's animals as well."

They waited silently at one side of the barn until the vet called them over. He explained that one of the puppies had died and was blocking the way for the others to be born. "It's a good job you called me when you did," he told them.

"Is the dog all right?" Laura asked him anxiously.

"She's fine now." He smiled at them. "And how's this for a Christmas present?" He pointed to two tiny puppies suckling from their mother.

"Oh, they're so sweet," said Emily.

"The black one's a boy and the sandy

one's a girl," said the vet.

"We should think of names for them," said Ben.

Laura looked at the contented trio on the straw. There was something special, magical even, about a birth on Christmas Eve. "How about Mary and Joseph?" she suggested.

"Brilliant!" they all agreed.

Later, the hospital phoned to say Mr Jakes had to stay in. Dad was home and he offered to drive them there so they could tell him about the puppies.

They arrived just as Mr Jakes came back from having an X-ray. He didn't look anything like so fierce, lying in a hospital bed. His leg was badly broken and he had to have an operation that evening.

"Your dog's fine," Laura told him. "She's had two lovely puppies."

"We've called them Mary and Joseph," said Emily. "Oh – unless you'd rather call them something else."

"No, they're good names," said Mr Jakes. "But the money for the vet," he turned towards Laura's dad. "I can't repay you."

"I haven't paid anything," said Dad. "What have you kids been saying?"

"It's all right, Dad. We're paying," said Ben. "The vet's sending his bill after Christmas."

"You're paying?" said the old man. "How?"

Between them, the children explained about Mr Crumbs, including the reason they'd wanted to use his barn.

"Why didn't you say that was why you needed the barn?" he asked.

"You didn't exactly give us a chance," said Sanjay.

"No, you're right, I'm sorry. But I get very twitchy about anyone going near the barn, because of the animals," said Mr Jakes. "Some of them have already been badly treated. The dog was chucked out on to the streets by her owner –

presumably because she was pregnant. And the fox was injured by boys throwing stones at it."

"We're not like that," said Ben indignantly.

"I know that now. And I'm so grateful to you for using your hard-earned money for my dog." Mr Jakes shifted uncomfortably in the bed. "But what about your pony? Where are you going to keep him?"

"We can't find anywhere," said Laura sadly.

"Well, providing you're going to look after him yourselves, he can live in my barn," said Mr Jakes. "I won't charge you anything."

"Wow!" said Laura, Emily and Sanjay together.

"It wouldn't be any good," said Ben quickly. "He's got to have at least an acre of field and you've got hardly any garden."

"The field out the back belongs to me," said Mr Jakes. "I bought it along with the farm cottage and the barn – it took all of my money. There was this donkey, you see – but she died before I could get her here…" His eyes misted over. "But it would be perfect for your pony."

Laura couldn't believe it. Mr Crumbs would be living just next-door! "Oh, that's brilliant! Thank you so much, Mr Jakes."

"Now steady on," said Dad. He'd gone quite pale. "You're going a bit fast here."

"But you promised!" Laura and Ben shouted at once.

"I didn't promise – I said I'd think about it," said Dad. "But I didn't really think—"

"You didn't think we could do it, did you?" said Laura. "But we have. We've got six months' money in advance and now we've got somewhere to keep him."

"Only we haven't got six months' money now," whispered Emily. "Not once we've paid the vet."

"Yes, we have," said Ben. "If we haven't got to pay any rent then we've got plenty of money." He whipped his calculator out.

"Without rent – for six months we only need about four hundred and sixty pounds to keep Mr Crumbs."

"And even if we have to pay the vet a hundred pounds, we've still got six hundred and two pounds and thirty-four pence left," said Laura.

"Oh, come on, give the kids a chance," said Mr Jakes. "What they've achieved is incredible. What are you worried about?"

"Money – I can't afford to bail them out if they get into difficulties. I've only just started up my business. And I'm sure Emily's mum—"

Mr Jakes beckoned Dad closer and whispered something to him.

As Dad listened, a smile gradually spread across his face.

"What?" said Laura.

Chapter 12

The Christmas Pony

"Happy Christmas, Mr Crumbs." Laura took out the carrot-shaped Christmas present.

"That's a bit obvious, isn't it?" laughed Emily.

Mr Crumbs pawed the snow-covered ground impatiently as Laura unwrapped it for him. It was a perfect Christmas day. Snow on the ground, but bright and crisp. And best of all – they now had their very own pony.

"I couldn't be more pleased," said Mrs Cox. "Fancy Mr Jakes coming up trumps like that. I'd never have thought of asking him."

"He's actually quite friendly when you get talking to him," said Ben. "And he knows loads about animals."

"And he doesn't look so old when he's not scowling," said Sanjay. "He's only been retired for a few years."

Mr Jakes had told them how he'd been taking in lost, unwanted and injured animals since he'd moved there six months ago. He'd tried to keep it a secret because he didn't want people poking round and frightening the animals.

"Did you find out what Mr Jakes

whispered to your dad to make him give in?" asked Sanjay.

"He pointed out that a pony and trap could be used for weddings," said Ben. "Dad's already worked out that it would be much cheaper than a second vintage car – which was what he was aiming towards."

"Mr Crumbs used to love pulling our old trap," said Mrs Cox. She stroked the pony's nose. "You'd enjoy doing that again, wouldn't you, Crumbs? Lots of company, lots of exercise."

"I still can't believe it," said Emily. "Mr Jakes was the last person I thought would have helped us. I thought –" She gave a giggle. "I thought he was a bank robber."

They all laughed.

Ben fastened the pony's New Zealand

rug on him to keep him warm and dry out in the snowy field.

"And we don't have to pay any rent, so we won't have to work so hard." Laura stroked Mr Crumbs's soft nose. "We'll be able to spend more time with you."

Mr Crumbs gave a soft whinny and tried to get in her pocket for the second hidden carrot.

Laura took it out and unwrapped it for him. They'd already decided to hold a Christmas bazaar every year and have a stall at the village summer fête. They still had to earn money, not only for Mr Crumbs's keep, but because they wanted to help with Mr Jakes's rescued animals too.

Laura gave Mr Crumbs another piece of carrot.

"He'll love it in the barn with all the

other animals," said Sanjay. "Especially when our dads have built his stall at one end."

"And I can leave without worrying now," said Mrs Cox. "Knowing that Mr Crumbs will be happy and well cared for. But I'm going to miss you all."

"We'll write to you – often," said Laura. "And let you know how Mr Crumbs is getting on."

The pony crunched on his carrot with his ears pricked, listening to them.

He gave a little snicker as Tiggy appeared and rubbed herself against his back leg. Then he put his soft muzzle into Laura's hand to see if he'd missed any bits of carrot.

She kissed him on his nose. "And you know what else, Crumbs? Tiggy's coming too. Mr Jakes said it's okay."

Ben patted Mr Crumbs's neck. "Mr Jakes is all right. He's just one of those people who gets on better with animals than with humans."

"But he wants us round there," said Laura. "And most important of all…" She reached up and whispered in Mr Crumbs's ear. "He wants you."

Mr Crumbs whinnied softly and rested his head on Laura's shoulder.

"Happy Christmas, everyone," said Laura, hugging him. "And a very special Happy Christmas to you, Mr Crumbs – our very own Christmas Pony."